This Little Tiger book belongs to:

logan W

To Bridie
A M

To Alice, with love
G W

LITTLE TIGER PRESS LTD,
an imprint of the Little Tiger Group
1 Coda Studios, 189 Munster Road,
London SW6 6AW
Imported into the EEA by
Penguin Random House Ireland,
Morrison Chambers, 32 Nassau Street,
Dublin D02 YH68
www.littletiger.co.uk

First published in Great Britain 1998
This edition published 2004
Text copyright © Alan MacDonald 1998
Illustrations copyright © Gwyneth Williamson 1998
Alan MacDonald and Gwyneth Williamson have
asserted their rights to be identified as the author
and illustrator of this work under the Copyright,
Designs and Patents Act, 1988
A CIP catalogue record for this book
is available from the British Library
All rights reserved
ISBN 978-1-84506-068-8
Printed in China
LTP/1800/3825/0621
6 7 8 9 10

BEWARE of the BEARS!

Alan MacDonald

Gwyneth Williamson

LITTLE TIGER

LONDON

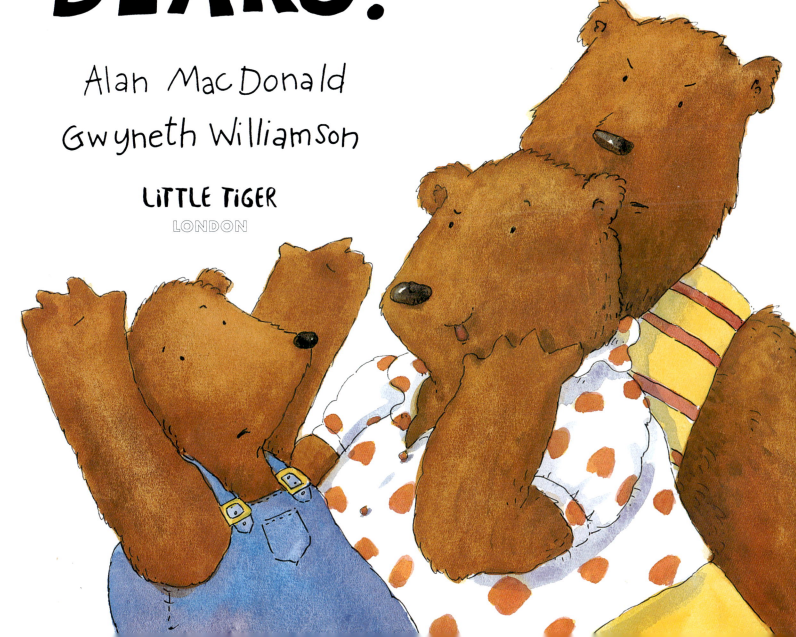

When the three bears saw what Goldilocks
had done to their little cottage, they were
hopping mad.

Their porridge eaten!

Chairs broken!

Beds bounced on!

"Go after her! Find out where she lives!"
ordered Daddy Bear.

Baby Bear jumped on
his scooter and sped
after Goldilocks.

In no time at all he was back.

"She lives on the far side of the forest," panted Baby Bear. "And what's more, she's just gone out again and left her door unlocked."

"Good!" said Mummy Bear. "What are we waiting for? Let's see how she likes having uninvited guests."

Baby Bear led the way through the
forest to Goldilocks' cottage. The door
was unlocked, just as he'd said.

On the breakfast table were several open packets.

"This isn't porridge," sniffed Mummy Bear.

Baby Bear read the labels. "Wheetos, Munch Flakes and Puffo Pops."

"Sounds all right to me," said Daddy Bear. "Pour away, Baby-o!"

"These Wheetos are too sweet," said Daddy Bear.
"These Munch Flakes are too noisy," said Mummy Bear.
"But these Puffo Pops are just right," said Baby Bear, catapulting a spoonful towards Daddy Bear.

A Puffo Pop hit Daddy Bear in the eye. He sent back
a spoonful of Wheetos. They splattered all over
Mummy Bear's best blouse.

   Soon cereal was flying left and right, till the carpet,
the walls and the ceiling were dripping with brown goo.

Baby Bear turned on the radio.
"Let's dance!" he squealed.

Mummy and
Daddy Bear
tangoed on
the table.
"This table's
too slippy," said
Daddy Bear.

They did the cha-cha round the curtains.
"These curtains are too rippy," said Mummy Bear.

"But this sofa's just right," squeaked Baby Bear, so they all jumped on the sofa and did the bossa nova until . . .

. . . they went right through it!

Next the three bears looked upstairs.
There were lots of things to try
in the bathroom.
"The shaving soap's too soapy,"
grumbled Daddy Bear.

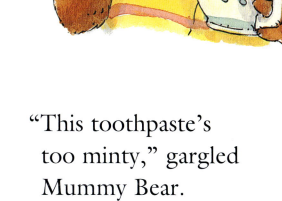

"This toothpaste's
too minty," gargled
Mummy Bear.

"But this bubble bath is
just right," murmured Baby
Bear from beneath a
mountain of suds.
"All right, here we come,"
said Mummy Bear . . .

They had a splashing
time in the bath
and . . .

. . . once they were clean and the bathroom a mess, off they went to the bedroom. "These pyjamas are too tight," said Daddy Bear, bursting the buttons. "This mattress is too lumpy," said Mummy Bear, bouncing up and down. "But these pillows are just right," said Baby Bear. "Just right for a pillow fight."

Baby Bear biffed Mummy Bear. Mummy Bear whacked Daddy Bear. Pillows burst, filling the air with clouds of feathers. Till suddenly Daddy Bear stopped.

"Listen!" he said. "I hear someone." Quietly, the three bears crept downstairs . . .

Goldilocks was in the kitchen.

Gleefully, Daddy Bear, Mummy Bear and Baby Bear watched from behind the door.

Goldilocks gasped when she saw the cereal splattered all over the walls.

Her eyes grew large when she saw the ripped curtains and the gigantic hole in the sofa.

She whistled when she saw the bathroom flooded with water and decorated with shaving foam.

Next Goldilocks went into the bedroom.
She stared open-mouthed at the sea of
feathers and the burst bedsprings.
Then suddenly the three bears jumped
out from behind the door.

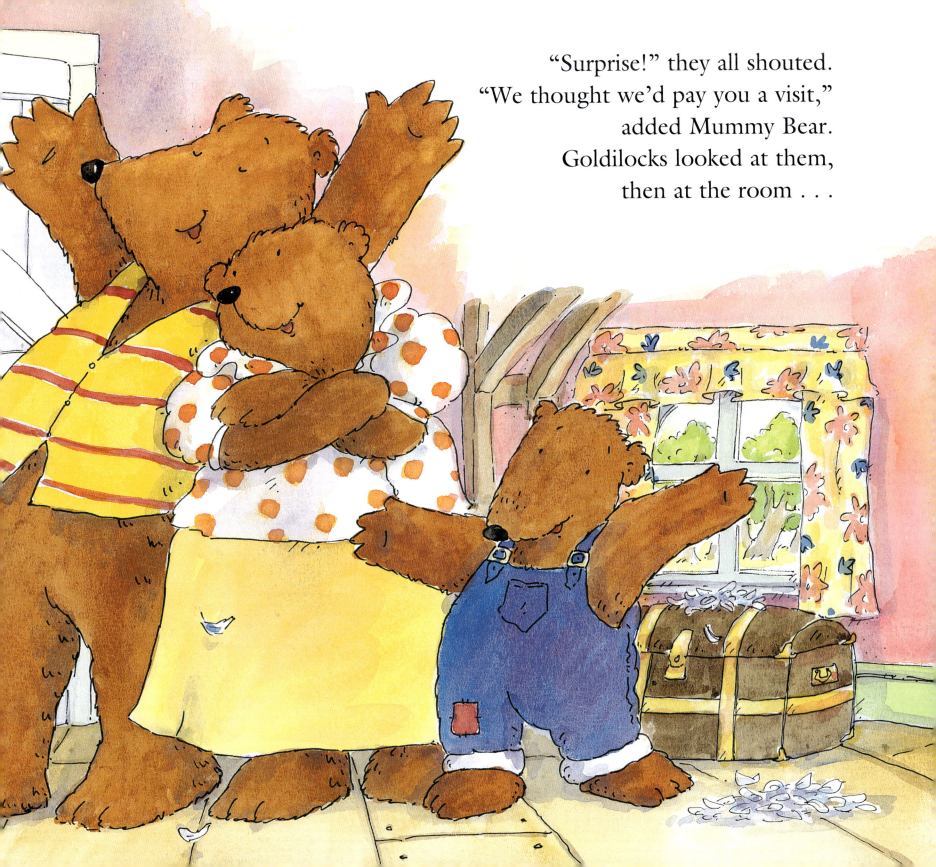

"Surprise!" they all shouted.
"We thought we'd pay you a visit,"
added Mummy Bear.
Goldilocks looked at them,
then at the room . . .

. . . and to the bears' astonishment, she threw back her head and laughed and laughed until her hair shook like golden springs.

"But aren't you mad at what we've done to your house?" asked Daddy Bear.

"My house? This isn't my house," giggled Goldilocks.

"But it must be," said Baby Bear, "I saw you go in."

"Oh that," said Goldilocks. "The door was open, so I thought I'd have a nose around. I'm always sneaking into other people's houses. I only came back because I left Teddy behind."

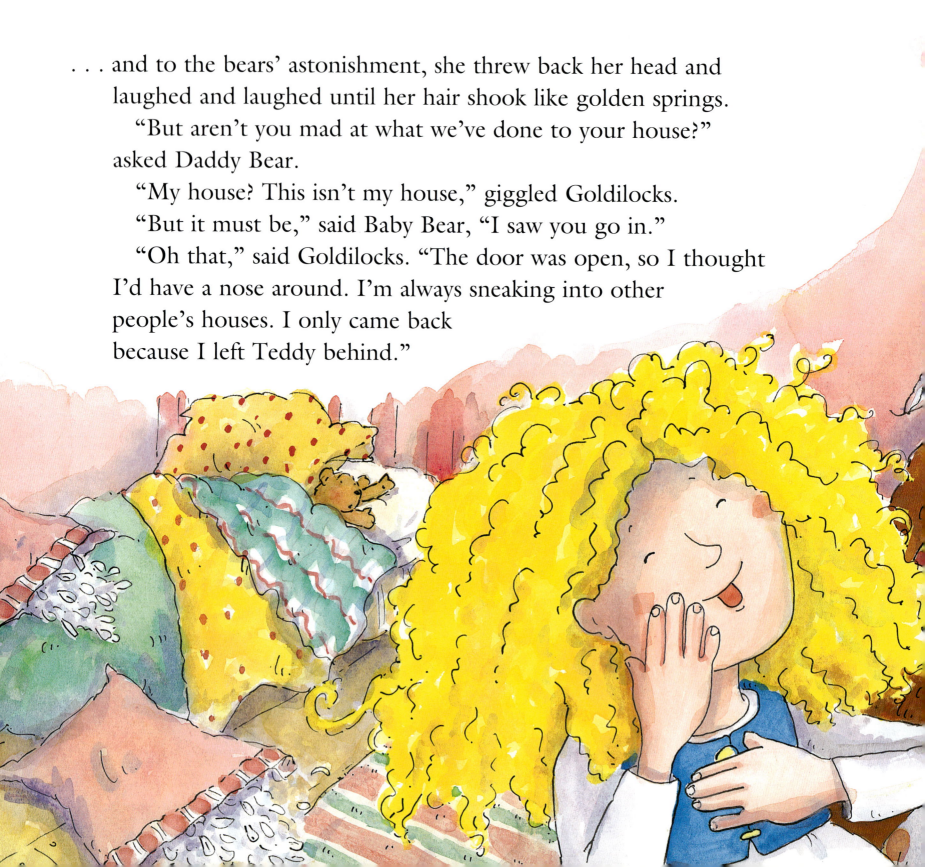

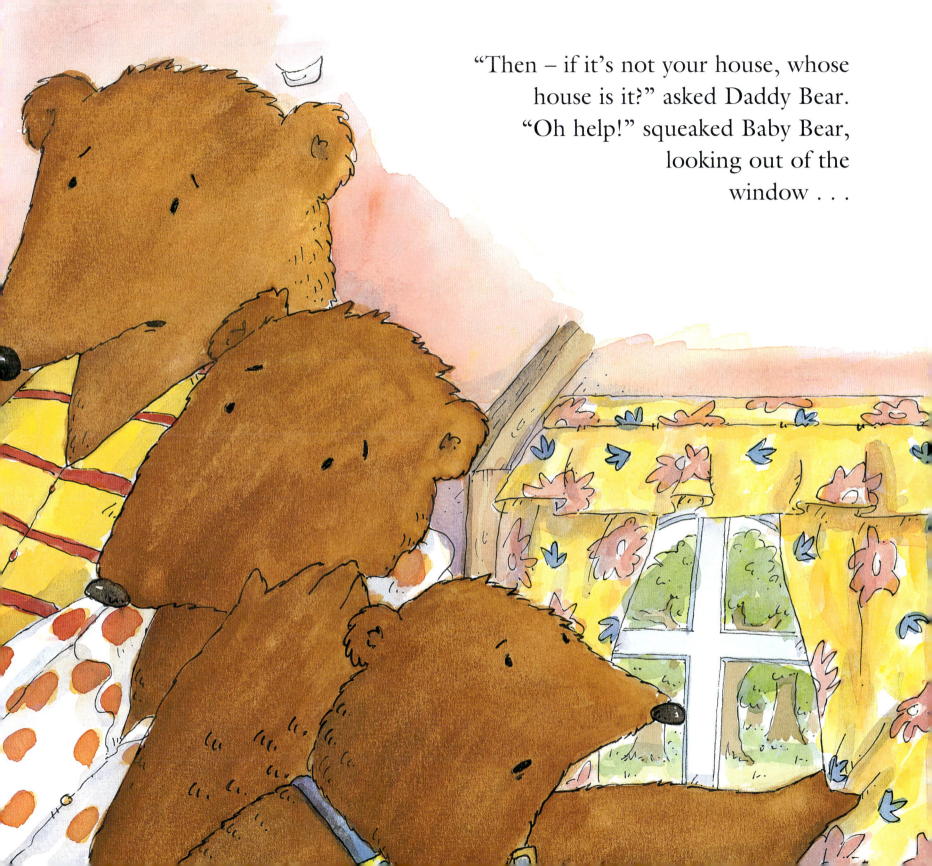

"Then – if it's not your house, whose house is it?" asked Daddy Bear. "Oh help!" squeaked Baby Bear, looking out of the window . . .